Monti Alto

Walter Hes

Johanna Tunks

Monti Alto

Many thanks to all who encouraged me.
Not every refugee story ends badly.
Walter Hes

Walter's fifth novel knits together a bundle of life stories into an exciting book. Born and raised in the Netherlands, Walter lived and worked with his family for nine years in South Africa, learning about refugee problems from several sides. He got to know and love the African people and their culture.

The readability of this book is mainly due to the dedication of the editor and dear family friend, the talented artist Hanny Tunks, who selflessly spent many hours editing his 'Dunglish'. She not only checked Walter's spelling and grammar but was so captivated by the story that she designed and painted the wonderful cover picture of the book.

Chapter One

It started so innocently. Ten school friends from Africa decided to leave their homeland and find a better life overseas, maybe in Europe or America. They did not have many luxuries at home, but some had a TV set where they could watch programs from overseas where, it seemed, everybody had cars and big houses. There were many restaurants, theatres and everything else anyone could wish for. At least, that was what it looked like to them.

They were smart young men and whilst they understood that those riches would depend on opportunities and working hard, they figured that those opportunities would be better and more abundant over there than here at home with its unpaved streets and where most houses were built with basket weave, timber and mud rather than with bricks and mortar.

Having grown up together, the ten friends had always been a close bunch, both at school and after. They all played in the soccer team, of which Paul was the captain. Addo, Joshua, Aron, Perry, Levy and Samuel were also school band members and played several kinds of instruments. They all would often get together, and nearly every time, their conversation would end up in dreaming the same dream about going to find a better life.

Now, finally, the decision was made. They planned their adventure as much as they could, and they saved all their pocket money. Paul and Monti, who had been in temporary jobs, had saved more than the others, but when the decision to go was made, they promised each other 'all for one and one for all'. It was agreed that Paul, who, as the captain of the soccer team, had already proven himself as such, would be best appointed as their leader. They also agreed that, where possible, they would not spend any of their savings until they had reached the sea.

Saying goodbye and leaving their families was hard. Some were leaving girlfriends behind as well. Benjamin, the youngest of the group, couldn't physically say goodbye to his mother, knowing she would cry, and then his father would make sure he could not go. He decided to leave them a note saying that he loved them and would never forget them.

After each of them had said their goodbyes to loved ones, they went on their way, not aware of what was to come. They were about to meet with hardship and hard work. They would be walking long distances, encounter dangerous situations and experience thirst, hunger and sometimes despair. Addo had brought his guitar along and would often lighten the atmosphere with a song or just some rhythm after a hard day to help restore the group's mood.

Their agreement of not spending money would prove somewhat idealistic. After all, what do you do when you have been living on only berries for three days? One does have to eat. The bow and arrow, which Samson made at one stage so they could hunt in the countryside, was confiscated at the first border post. They would find out that there was no choice but to buy food, which was to be mostly bread, in addition to some chicken and greens to make a reasonably nutritious soup with the bread to add some bulk to their stomachs.

They had never realised before how big Africa was and how enormous the distances were, especially by foot. Things were about to become particularly tricky with one of the boys being kidnapped, and a significant and dangerous rescue action was required.

Chapter Two

After a long hike, the ten friends arrived at a big river and were looking forward to a refreshing dip in the water. The river was wide and calm but looked like it could be occupied by hungry crocodiles. They walked further downstream to where the river was much narrower, but its current ran much faster.

Benjamin, Monti and Levy took their clothes off and tried the water whilst the others sat down to rest. When Benjamin moved too far from the edge, he was taken by the strong current. Despite being so well-built and strong, he couldn't prevent being swept further away. Monti and Levy shouted alarm to the group, but Ben was too far downstream already.

Not sure what to do, they all ran down along the riverbank just when a yacht came downstream and stopped. They were relieved to see that the people on the yacht were fishing Benjamin out of the water but to everyone's disbelief, he was not put on land! Then the yacht steamed away at full speed with Ben on board. Paul could just read the name of the yacht, 'The River Queen'.

Frustrated and concerned about their friend, the group walked further along the water's edge until they ran into some people. They were friendly locals, and when asking them about the yacht, one of them replied, "Oh that belongs to the queen. She lives on the other side of the river a bit further downstream." The friendly people went on to say that the woman had been the wife of the King, but because she had an insatiable sexual appetite and the poor man was unable to keep up with her, he sent her as far away as he could. Young Benjamin was probably taken to make him the Queen's sex slave.

So now, in order to rescue their friend, the group needed to get to the other side of the river and find the queen's residence. "Can we cross the river here somewhere?" Paul asked. "No," was the reply, "It will only get wider, and the current is too strong this time of the year". Paul, a quick thinker, had a solution to that problem and said, "Okay, so we need to find someone to take us to the other side of the river or buy some rope long enough to span the width of the river for each of us to hold on to and help us to cross".

The friendly locals directed them to a little fishing village further down the river. Paul thanked them, and the group went down to the village. After asking around but failing to find someone who could take them across, they bought a long rope and walked back to where the river was at its narrowest.

Their first trial to cross the river was nearly a disaster. The current was just too strong, and the rope turned out to be about five or six metres too short, as Monti would soon find out. Being the strongest swimmer, he attempted to take the rope to the other side. Firmly holding on to it, he started to swim across the river, but with the current so strong and the rope too short, Monti was not going to make it to the other side. He was desperately hanging on the rope halfway across the river, and his friends had to pull him back. Now what? They had to come up with a new plan.

Samson walked a few yards upstream into the bush, and whilst swinging like a monkey on a long liana, he yelled out, "If we cut this liana up there, and we tie it to the rope, it will be long enough to span the river." One of them cut the liana on one side, and another tested the other side to make sure it was attached securely enough for its purpose. They tied a long piece of the liana onto the rope, which should now be of sufficient length to span the river. They decided that this time, two men should try to cross.

This time, Samson, who was a good swimmer too, joined Monti for a second attempt to get the rope, which was now lengthened with the liana, to the other side. When they reached halfway, they used the current to help them float to the other side whilst holding onto the rope. Even for strong swimmers, this was a struggle.

After catching their breath, they searched for a substantial tree stump. When they found one, they tied the rope to it. Now, they had a bridge. Firmly holding on to the rope and with their clothes bundled on top of their heads, they crossed over to the other side, one by one. There wasn't much time to rest, especially not for the last ones arriving. Without any time to waste, they had to go back down the river to find the house, locate Benjamin and get him back. They left the rope behind for the monkeys.

Chapter Three

It was a long way back again before they saw the big house or rather the mansion of 'the Queen'. Around the house was a big fence with barbed wire on top. There was a kind of canal, where the yacht was berthed, with a partly separate fenced laneway to the house. The canal had a big steel fence and gate, which was securely locked.

It was decided that Addo, Joshua, Levy and Perry would walk around the fence to the back of the house to check if they could get in somewhere. Then, by using their secret bird song whistle, which would hopefully be heard and answered by Ben, find out where he was held. Paul, Monti, Samson, Revel and Aron were going to try and get into the property from the front and saw only one possibility, which was to try and swim under the gate to get onto the grounds. Monti and Samson dove into the canal first to check that possibility. Fortunately, the gate did not reach the bottom so, surfacing on the other side, Samson gave Paul and the others the thumbs up to follow him and Monti. After passing their clothes through the fence, they all dove in and swam under the gate, ending up inside the grounds.

They went to the house, where they found the front doors unlocked. Samson, followed by the others, walked in as if he belonged there. A guard, who looked half asleep, was sitting behind a desk, and before he knew it, he received a smash against his head. They tied his arms to his back with his belt and his feet with his own shoelaces. They didn't think to put anything in his mouth, so the guard was able to let out a loud yell when he came around, alerting the soldiers.

There was a set of double doors, each door with a nice big pot plant on a stand next to it. Two soldiers barged through the doors. Paul and Monti knocked them out, each with one of the pot plants. Now, the coast was clear to go and rescue young Benjamin. When their secret bird call whistle was returned, they knew they had located Benjamin's whereabouts in the building. They were lucky that the key was in the door and there were no guards nearby or inside.

Levy, Addo, Joshua and Perry went around and found a steel grid, covering a recently filled hole in the ground inside the fence. Levy and Addo started digging with their hands, even without tools, which was easier than expected because the ground was still soft from the recent backfill. Joshua and Perry continued along the fence to investigate further but ran back pretty quickly when they heard their friend scream, "Stop!!!" Levy, who, after succeeding to make a big enough hole and passing through under the fence, threw away the grid, screaming, "There are wild hogs inside the fence!!"

They knew that wild pigs were more dangerous than guard dogs. Wild pigs attack anything and rip it apart with their sharp tusks. They eat anything, live or dead. Levy, who had just managed to get through, heard them coming and never did a human come as fast through a small opening as Levy did from under that fence. Once through, he immediately pressed himself against the fence outside the hole. They all stood like statues of fright, but what nobody believed possible, happened. At full speed, all the hogs went through the hole and to freedom into the forest without hurting anyone.

Hoping there would be no other animals, the boys crawled under the fence and onto the grounds. They walked up to the front via the side of the house where, earlier, their bird call sign had been answered. As they now had a rough idea of where Benjamin was being held, they went to the front to tell the others how they got in and that Benjamin was somewhere on the right side of the house.

As it turned out, Addo and his two companions beat them to it and had already freed Ben. Again complete, the ten friends ran around to the hole in the fence and disappeared into the bush as the hogs had done before them.

Meanwhile, the queen's loyal soldiers were surrounding the untied yacht, thinking the intruders wanted to leave by boat. This was precisely what Paul expected, and he had told the group to throw off the yacht's mooring lines before they entered the grounds.

Chapter Four

After many detours and other delays, they arrived at a huge savannah. Though there weren't many trees, they couldn't see the other side. The savannah had appeared unexpectedly, and they felt they needed to go back to the stream to fill their water bottles, before they did the big trek, thinking it was best not to rely on the possibility that there would be a waterhole somewhere.

The enormous flat land looked like an ocean, with the wind moving the grass like waves. In some places, the grass was nearly as tall as a man. With the wind in their back, they enjoyed their relatively easy walk.

Suddenly, there was a mighty roar that could only have come from a giant lion. Samson quickly grabbed his bow and arrows. Five others were carrying the six-foot-long bamboo sticks with sharp ends they had made. Paul and Monti quickly put them in the defence lines, two at the front and three at the back. Some questioned this strategy, but Monti said, "You do know that lions hunt in a pack, right? We need to watch our backs. There may be more than one lion out there!"

So, Benjamin and Aron, closely followed by Samson with his bow and arrows, were in the frontline with Levy, Joshua and

Perry in the back. The group slowly kept walking. They could smell the lion before they saw him in the long grass. It was a big, fierce animal, but he soon gave way to the ten determined young men with spears and loud shouts. Addo, who was in the centre of the group with Revel, Paul and Monti, had taken his guitar from his back, and instead of using it as a weapon, he played a few notes. To everyone's surprise and relief, the lion bolted in the opposite direction! Afterwards, Addo would often boast that he chased the lion away. They all agreed with him. Out of sheer fear, Addo had played so many false notes, that the animal could not stand it and disappeared. Feeling a sense of pride and achievement after their adventures so far, the group continued on their trek, but it wasn't going to be plain sailing. Whilst it was a relatively easy walk through the savanna, they could easily lose each other in the man-high grass. But if that were to happen, they'd have their special bird call to locate each other. Often, the terrain took them in the wrong direction. It also became quite hot around the middle of the day, but they kept going because there were no trees to give them some shade.

Towards the end of the afternoon, they reached the end of the savannah and were back in the bush. They stopped to rest for a while but then pushed on until they arrived at a crossroad that ran exactly East-West. They decided to go West.

After a while, the group came to a small village. They saw a man working on his land and asked him where they could get some water and maybe food. The farmer said there were no shops around here but that he could use some help on his farm if the group were after some work. Tired from a day of walking but interested, the group introduced themselves and sat down on the ground to chat.

The farmer, whose name was Joseph, wondered by himself if he could get some of those strong and good-looking young men hooked up with each of his four daughters. He could use some extra hands on his farm permanently, and he suggested to the friends that they could stay on his property if they would like to help him to turn over the land so he could sow his corn, or 'mielies', as it is called in South Africa.

They made a deal, and the friends were in for a good time. Joseph's daughters cooked for ten extra young men, and there was quite a bit of flirting going on. There weren't enough tools at the farm for ten men, so Joseph went and borrowed some of his neighbours. Even so, there still was only enough equipment for half of them, so the group took turns working and playing. The young men thoroughly enjoyed their time with Joseph and his daughters, but one day, when most of the work was done, the group decided it was time to go. Joseph and his daughters were sad to see them go, but the land was done, and the mielies were in the ground.

Refreshed, the friends were on their way again, but there were many more obstacles to overcome on their journey on foot. Occasionally, they would try to get a lift, but that was not always easy because they were with so many and didn't want to be separated. They felt they needed to stay together as a group as much as possible. Sometimes, some of them would manage to find casual jobs here and there to boost their savings, but the money would never last long with ten mouths to feed.

One time, when the group tried to cross one of the borders, they were apprehended and detained by the local authorities because, without any papers, they couldn't identify themselves. Their handmade spears and Addo's bow and arrows were confiscated and never returned. Without passports or other identification, it took long, exhausting interrogations, legalities and pleading as well as a big chunk out of their savings, after which they finally were given three days to depart the country, or they would be kept in detention as illegal immigrants indefinitely. They did not need to be told twice. They made themselves scarce, continuing on their journey, as quickly as they could!

Chapter Five

Close to two months later, the group eventually reached the desert. Someone told them that this desert was about a thousand miles wide and about five times as long! They knew then that walking across it was not an option. The bush was something they were used to, but a desert was quite something else. Even so, they had to cross the desert to get to the sea, and they decided that they needed to find someone with transport who would be willing to take them across for as much of the way as possible.

After many desperate searches and enquiries, they managed to get a truck driver to take them for most of the way. After some hours in the truck, the driver dropped them off. "You look like fit young men", he said, "If you walk in a straight line, you could cross the desert and reach the sea in about four to five hours". Even though they would have to walk a fair bit, it was decided that it could be done. The group thanked the man and went on their way. They would, however, find out that the truck driver's opinion about that time frame had been just a tad optimistic.

The group had sufficient water with them, or so they thought, and they started the walk in good spirits. When they took their first break, they remembered the truck driver's advice to walk the desert in a straight line. After discussing this, and because they didn't have a compass, they came up with a method to do that. They would use their wristwatch and the sun.

Using the watch as a compass, they first determined where the North was. Addo and Levy started to walk in the right direction. Then, one of them stopped and waited while the second one walked a bit further. The group then indicated when the second one was in the right line. Next, the whole group would walk past, and the one who was first was now last. Repeating this system would keep them in line by waving left or right to the person going forward. It was slow going, but at least they knew they were on the right track.

But after a while, water became scarce, and some of them had nothing left. It was hot, very hot, and the weaker guys needed a lot of encouragement from the stronger ones. Their mouths had become very dry, and their tongues swollen, making it difficult to talk for even the strongest of them. They needed all their energy to keep walking. The straight-line system had not been followed for some time now because they were so exhausted. Some of them were close to giving up, desperate and thinking, "What have we done? Are we going to die here in this horrible desert?"

Just as they were wondering if it would have been better to have stayed at home and lived, they heard Samson, who, from the top of a sand dune, was shouting out, "There's the sea guys, there's the sea!!" At long last, and barely alive after their horrid experience, they arrived at what they hoped was the Mediterranean coast. Their ordeal in the desert was behind them. They survived! The relief was enough to give everyone the energy to go further and keep going.

At the first road sign, they saw that Tripoli was twelve kilometres away. They had indeed ended up on the Mediterranean coast. Considering their not completely recovered condition, twelve kilometres was still a long way by foot, but they kept going. Luckily, the group soon ran into some kind people who gave them water to drink. After the young men told them about their ordeal and where they were headed, the well-meaning people gave them some good advice.

The friends were advised not to hang around in the city during the evening or at night. "The police will pick you up with nasty consequences", the young men were told, and that they should make sure to get to the harbour site very early in the morning for the best chance to get some paid work. "That way, you can take your time to look out for someone who can take you to Italy but be aware of 'middlemen' who promise you the world, take your money and disappear, never to be seen again!"

After some rest and rehydration, the young men felt reasonably refreshed, and the group were optimistic once more. They went on their way again and soon found a reasonable place to stay for the night. The next day, following the good advice from the well-meaning people, they made sure to be at the docks at first daylight, and it wasn't hard to find daily casual work at the docks. They also found a small bazaar where food was not too expensive. Having paid work, they didn't need to touch their savings to get by. They even boosted their savings some more with the money made at the docks. Now it was time to find someone with a boat who would be willing to take them to Italy and they would find out the hard way that there were more sharks on the land than there were in the sea.

Chapter Six

Whilst enquiring about a passage to Italy, the friends were told great stories and even promises of work were made. They received offers that seemed too good, and because the group was warned that this would happen, they were careful and decided they would check a bit further. After discussion as to how to go about it, they all agreed that Monti and Paul, who were the most mature-looking of the group, were the best candidates to go and look for the middle-man who had made those offers. They both used to have jobs back home and spoke English a little.

Pretending to be journalists for a well-known newspaper wanting to learn more about the trade of trafficking people to Europe, they went looking for the man. But when they found him, the man was adamant that he had nothing to do with the trade and was just passing by. "You must have mistaken me for somebody else", he said, turning around and disappearing into the crowd. This experience convinced them that all these traders just wanted their money and wouldn't care about what could happen to them at sea. Monti and Paul reported back to the group with the conclusion that this was yet another reason to keep their wits about them and check things out before paying anyone.

Eventually, the friends heard about a young Italian man who was willing to take them to Italy for a reasonable amount. It was a small boat with only this man as captain and one other sailor, so the friends were expected to help on board. They were, however required to pay for the passage up front. With everything organised, they would leave Africa the next evening.

Paul, whose parents had Italian friends and he'd learned to speak a little Italian in his childhood, explained as best as he could that he would be happy to pay upfront for the groups' passage if they could stay on board for the night. "No," the captain said, "that is too dangerous." He went on to say that if the local police got wind of that, they would arrest them and send them back to where they came from. Paul agreed but said that in that case, they were not going to pay upfront. The captain, in turn, could not accept that because he needed money upfront to buy fuel and supplies for the journey. Paul and the others thought that was fair enough, and it was agreed they would pay him some money up front and the remainder when boarding.

After dark the next evening, the group boarded the small boat to take them across to Italy. Three more families with small children were already on board. The trip to the mainland was rough but could have been much worse as only half the population on board had been seasick. Anyone who was well enough had to help as much as they could with small things like distributing food and water and cleaning up the mess. When land appeared in the far distance, every-one was so happy and relieved that they would get off this boat very soon now, only to be disappointed by the captain's announcement that they had to go further North and wait until dark before they could dock. Slowly, they drifted closer to land. Suddenly, a big yacht hailed them and came alongside them. The captain of the yacht jumped on board their boat, and then there was quite a bit of shouting going on. Paul, with his limited knowledge of the Italian language, could only make out some words about things that would become clearer after it was too late. Unbeknownst to everyone on the boat, their captain and the captain of the big yacht were brothers and the sons of the big mafia boss. The mafia had just declared that they would not handle the refugee trade, and when Pa found out what his youngest son was up to, he sent his eldest son to stop him with the order to "Make damn sure he does as I say!"

The captain returned to his passengers, telling them they had to wait until dark and that everybody should give him their papers. He told them that the papers were needed by the people on the yacht who were going to bribe the local police so that they could safely land later. He then went on board the yacht with the passengers' papers, and two other men with automatic guns in their hands jumped from the yacht onto the small boat. They went to the back and shot a burst of holes in the bottom. They did the same in the middle and again in the front before they jumped back on board the yacht.

Everyone on board the small vessel was in a panic, and while they frantically tried to stop the seawater from rushing into the boat, the yacht took off quickly. It was no use. Their boat was doomed, and all they could think of was to go and try to swim to shore. The mothers were screaming and pleading to please save their kids.

Monti and Samson each took a child and jumped into the sea, but the children couldn't swim and were panicking, clinging to their rescuers and restricting their movements. Samson soon found himself in difficulty, and he became separated from his child. Monti quickly grabbed the child and held on to that one as well, but the children were clinging to him so tight that even Monti, despite being such a strong swimmer, couldn't swim anymore. The friends made it to shore safely, except Samson and Monti. Samson had to be dragged out of the water, and with great difficulty, they eventually got Monti out as well, but he was unconscious and not breathing. One of them, who knew first aid, performed CPR on him and turned him on his side, enabling a large amount of water to drain from his mouth and nose. Then Monti coughed and sat up. "How are the kids?" was the first thing he asked, but sadly, his friends could only give him the bad news.

Chapter Seven

From all on board of the wrecked boat, it seemed the ten friends were the only ones who made it to land. When Monti came to, he insisted he wanted to go back into the sea and search for the kids. It took a lot of persuasion from the others to get him to go with them, away from the shore.

They travelled further inland, mainly in the dark of the night, until Monti became too sick and could go no further. Along the road and not far from a little village, they found two little open sheds with some straw for animals. They decided to stay there at least until Monti was better.

The next day Paul decided that, because he was the only one with some knowledge of the Italian language, he would go to the nearby village to find work. To his delight, the first little restaurant or bistro he saw had a sign advertising for a waiter position. The bistro owner was a bossy, loud and fast-talking woman cursing a lot, and Paul, with his limited knowledge of Italian, could make neither head nor tail of what she was saying.

Then, a young African girl passed by the bistro. "Hi, I am Ozie," she said with a big white smile, "Can I be of any help?" She was naturally beautiful with big brown eyes and glowing dark skin. Paul couldn't stop staring at her. "Yes....um.... I'm Paul", he stammered, "Err...do you speak Italian at all?" Yes, she did. Ozie had been in the country for some years and worked for a wealthy family in the village not far from the restaurant. With enough knowledge of the language, she was able to translate for Paul and the boss lady. Paul quickly agreed to all the things the boss wanted him to do and got the job.

Ozie took an instant liking to Paul and would often pass by the bistro. Paul, who had not been able to put her out of his mind since he first set eyes on her, made it a habit to take extra time to clean the tables outside the bistro, especially around the time that Ozie would walk past. Her beautiful face, with those huge dark brown eyes, generous mouth and pitch black long hair in braids framing her face, appeared in his dreams, but she was always out of reach.

Whenever Ozie walked past, she'd always answered his greeting, often stopping for a chat. They had easy conversations, like they knew each other for a long time. She came from a different area than he and his mates, but language was no problem as they both spoke Swahili as well as English. The two often went for walks after Paul finished work.

Eventually, Paul told Ozie his story about how he and his friends ended up here in Italy. When he told her about how they tried to rescue the children and what had happened to Monti, her big brown eyes filled up with tears. When Paul put his arms around her to comfort her, Ozie looked up to him and kissed him. Paul responded passionately, and he realised that the reason for wanting to stay in this area was not only his sick friend Monti. He wanted to stay with this girl just as much.

Chapter Eight

Jack and Susan had been farming in Southern Africa for many years. They had a dream of travelling around the world and possibly settling in Italy and often talked about it. When they received an offer to sell their farm, it provided the opportunity to go and realise their dream.

Jack, a man of six foot three, muscular and lean, grew up on a farm and was used to the hard work. Susan was an attractive woman with blond hair, and a head shorter than Jack. She was a music teacher when she fell for him all those years ago. They didn't have children, and Susan had adapted wonderfully to the farming lifestyle and the hard work that comes with it. The offer that had been made for their immaculately maintained farm was very good, so they decided to sell now before they would be too old to maintain it or their circumstances changed. They sold the farm, but it was not possible to get that much money out of the country at once, and a solution needed to be found. Fortunately, it so happened that a good friend of the couple was the bank manager with one of the bigger banks, and they were able to come to an arrangement. Jack and Susan would be able to each take a lump sum now and the bank would send them an agreed and ample amount each, as their monthly pension.

Off they went on their, long-dreamed about, holiday travelling around Europe. After a while and having seen quite a bit of Europe by now, they were travelling around Italy. They were no longer interested in all the hustle and bustle of tourist places. They liked Italy, especially its countryside. For them, the cities were too busy, too noisy and too smelly, so the decision was made that they would buy a home somewhere in Italy's countryside. They visited several real estate agents with no luck so far. Then, one day, on one of such visits, they found out that there were sometimes whole mountain villages for sale at very low prices, and they started to visit several of those so-called ghost villages. They became enthusiastic about the idea. It was like finding a new hobby.

When, on one of their trips, Jack and Susan, came to a small village, they found out that, a little further up the mountain, there was one such ghost village. They only had a quick look from a distance that day because their hired car refused to get up the terraced track leading up to the old village, so they decided they would get up early the next day to try and have a closer look.

The small hotel where they were staying was basic but clean, and the people were very friendly. But the bed looked uncomfortable, and Jack remarked that he would have to throw the mattress on the floor if he wanted to walk straight up the next morning. Later that afternoon, they went for a walk and decided to go for a drink at a tiny little bistro at the end of town. They were discussing the mountain village when the waiter came, asking them if they would like a drink or something to eat. The waiter was Paul

Overhearing Jack and Susan's conversation, Paul said in Swahili/ English that they sounded like they came from his country. They all thought that this was a nice coincidence. Paul felt quite at ease chatting with Jack and Susan, who soon explained where they were from, and this was not too far from where Paul had grown up. After taking Jack's order for beer, he quickly came back with the drinks and asked if they would like to order the Lasagna for the misses and a Spaghetti Bolognese for the boss.

"Why are you so adamant about us ordering this food specifically, or is that the only choice on the menu?" Jack asked.

"Sir, firstly, it is because the Padrona can't cook many things very well except pasta. Secondly, she always cooks a lot of it, and then I can take the leftovers to my friends". There were no other customers as yet, so Paul was able to tell Jack and Susan some of his story and how he and nine other men were hiding in the sheds just outside the village. He told them that he was the only one who was able to get them food.

"Are you guys illegal immigrants?" Susan asked. "Yes, I guess according to the law, we are, but that is a long story", Paul answered with a worried look on his face. "At the moment, we can't walk into the village, or the police will probably pick us up. We can't move anywhere else because one of us is sick."

When the food was served, Jack and Susan ate enough to be satisfied. It was good and wholesome food, and they left plenty for Paul to take to his friends. They promised him they would see what they could bring to help his friends and come back tomorrow.

Chapter Nine

Back at their hotel, Jack and Susan enquired about the deserted mountain village and whom they should see for more information. "You will have to speak to the mayor, signor Don Giovani", the hotel receptionist told them. "And where can we find Mr Giovani?" They were told that in the mornings, The Don normally is in the Town Hall, in the afternoon, after siesta, he'll be in his building yards and towards the evening, he could be found in the cafe or the bakery.

The next morning, Paul and Susan walked through the town and asked at the bakery. No Don Giovani there and no luck at the town hall either. They eventually got a hold of him in his hardware store and building supply yards. After the introduction, The Don said, "So you are interested in old Valparaiso?" "If that is the mountain village that's up for sale, yes we are", Susan said. "You are now in Novo Valparaiso, and the one on the mountain is called Valparaiso Vecchio or old Valparaiso", The Don said. Fortunately for Jack and Susan, Don Giovani spoke reasonable English as their Italian was still very limited.

Don Giovanni invited them for a cappuccino in his café and there Jack and Susan found out that he owned half the town. He explained some of the facts about the old village and that most of the young people had left for the big city. "The village is not accessible with a normal automobile", he said. "Yes, we found that out yesterday," Jack answered. "Not only is the road steep but also very narrow in some places". Don suggested that they borrow the small four-wheel truck he had in the yard if Jack could drive it. Jack thanked him for the offer and told the Don that they used to have a big farm, and that they certainly were capable of driving all kinds of vehicles, so he did not expect any problems.

The Don further explained that the village had been abandoned for a long time and that finding all the owners would not be easy. Jack and Susan didn't expect things to go easy. They were becoming well aware that they rarely do. But at least, having been given a loan of the Don's old truck, they could drive up to the village. They wouldn't have to climb up the steps the last couple of hundred metres and need not to be as worried about a few scratches on the car as they had been with their hired car.

The following day, after a fitful night's sleep on the mattress on the floor, they went up to the ghost village of Valparaiso Vecchio. The first impression from a distance was quite interesting but coming closer they saw broken houses and some roofs had collapsed. They counted nine small houses and one bigger one next to the church. The church doors were solidly locked. From the house next to the church, which was in a better condition than the others, Susan called Jack. "Come and have a look at the beautiful view, she said excitedly. "I want big windows here to see it all day!" Jack said, "Steady now, we are not living here yet, not by a long shot."

The houses were built around the small square which was in front of the church. There was also a kind of pond with a fountain. It was almost completely overgrown and had no water. The bigger house had three rooms, including one large one with a nice view. The kitchen even had some furniture in it. They didn't stay long as they only went up there for a first impression after all. Jack thought it quite sad seeing the dilapidated houses, and he remarked that the owners could never ask much for this lot.

Back down in the little town of Novo Valparaiso, Jack and Susan returned the truck but did not see the Don. They then went to buy some chocolate bars for the boys and, later on, some bread and other things at the bakery. After they got back to their hotel, they decided to have an aperitif there before going for a stroll to the small restaurant for dinner where Paul was awaiting them. He brought them some drinks straight away.

Jack ordered the same food as before, and Susan pointed Paul to the bag with the goodies she had brought for his friends. Paul was grateful, but right now he was very worried about Monti, who had deteriorated and was very ill.

Chapter Ten

After another restful night on the mattress on the floor in their hotel, Jack and Susan left for the big harbour town. On the way they discussed how they would be able to get hold of some good antibiotics. Last night, Paul told them that Monti, his friend who nearly drowned, was now very sick with a high fever and asked if there was any way they could get some antibiotics for him.

Susan had promised Paul that they would see what they could do for Monti. "Please don't try the local doctor", Paul had stressed because Ozie told him that this doctor would not prescribe anything without seeing the patient, and Jack concluded that this meant that they had to go to the big harbour town again. Susan responded with glee, "Oh well, we can do some more shopping whilst there". To her, any excuse to go shopping in the big town was a good one.

When they arrived in the big harbour town, they tried an apothecary, but without a prescription from a doctor, they could not be of any help. When they went to an 'informazione publican to find a doctor, they were told that they would have to make an appointment and would probably not be seen the same day or even the next.

After further searching, they located a doctor at an expensive-looking address with a big house with a brass plate and decided to try their luck there. Upon entering, they found a nice-looking, friendly receptionist sitting at her desk in the lobby. She even spoke English. She asked how she could help them. Jack and Susan had made up a story that they were in the harbour with their yacht and that one of the men on board was very sick. The receptionist told them yes, they could see the doctor but they must pay for the consultancy fee up front. They paid and the young lady went with them to see the doctor and translated for them. The result was a prescription for strong antibiotics.

They went to the apothecary, paid for and picked up the medication. They then went for a stroll through town, walking along the harbour side and through the shopping mall where, at a supermarket, they bought a big supply of food and other things for the boys. It would have been too obvious and could raise suspicion if they bought in those amounts at the shop in the little village.

On their way to the back Jack and Susan took a detour and saw Paul walking to town as they had hoped. Paul asked them to turn around and park a bit further along behind some bushes. On the other side of the road were the two small open huts where the boys were staying. They parked the car and took the medicines, water and some of the food. They waited for any traffic to pass, then crossed the road and met up with the rest of the boys in the hut where Monti was.

At night, Paul, together with Ben, Samson and Levy, stayed with Monti. The other five slept in the other hut. It was a bad situation. Monti was very ill indeed and had a high fever. With a bottle of fresh water, Susan got some antibiotics into him. That evening, Jack and Susan discussed with the group of friends what the best way to help them would be. It was difficult now that Monti was so ill. Susan suggested that the boys would be best off in the village up the mountain. They all agreed.

Jack realised he would have to talk to the Don in order to get things moving. "We'll go and see Mr Giovanni tomorrow, and if it works out, we will have a nice labour force to help renovate and redevelop the village", he said. "Bah," Susan said, "Do men always have to think about that kind of thing first? What about these poor boys?" Jack responded that he was only being practical. "I bet the boys will be keen to work for a roof over their head and shared food, won't you guys?" They nodded enthusiastically. "We'll take good care of the them", he reassured her.

Susan was particularly concerned about Monti after seeing him lie there in that open hut on just a bit of straw. The next morning, she took the sheets of their bed in the hotel with the plan to go and bring them to the boys' shelter for Monti. She would later explain to the matron of the small hotel that they had a little accident that night and ruined the bed sheets but for the matron not to worry and that no one needs to know because she was going to get rid of the ruined ones and buy new sheets to replace them as soon as possible.

That same morning and with the sheets from their bed they drove around the little town and, coming from the other side, dropped them off at the boys' hideaway for Monti, hoping that he would be more comfortable now that he would not have to lie there on straw only. Then they went to see the Don to talk about the purchase of Valparaiso and the possibility of moving into the mountain village as soon as possible.

Chapter Eleven

Jack and Susan had a long conversation with Don Giovani. Jack explained that they had finances and wanted to buy Valparaiso but also move up there as soon as possible. "Signore, please understand that we have lived in hotels for months," Jack said, "Not that there's anything wrong with the one we are staying in now", he continued, hastily explaining that he and Susan just wanted to get settled now, make their own home and be in their own place.

The local bank manager was a good friend of the Don, and if Jack and Susan could convince his friend that they had sufficient funds, it was fine to move up there as far as he was concerned. Don Giovanni accompanied Jack and Susan to the bank, where he introduced them to his friend, the bank manager. "I shall go now," the Don said. But Jack, wanting him to stay, said, "Signore, when we succeed in the purchase of Valparaiso Vecchio, we are going to need you very often for building materials and other things. Please stay, we like you to hear what the bank manager thinks about our financial situation".

Jack explained to both men that they sold their farm back in southern Africa but could not bring all their money out of the country at once, and an arrangement was made that he and Susan each would receive an ample sum of money each every month. "We can easily take care of all our commitments", Jack said, turning to the bank manager, "please check our credentials".

The bank manager said he would and he pre-approved Jack and Susan on the condition that it would indeed all check out. Don Giovani agreed with the amount of the deposit. Jack and Susan could move temporarily into their village, and the Don would make sure that the paperwork was done as soon as possible. Afterwards, Don Giovanni accompanied Jack and Susan back to his building material shop where they bought the first lot of supplies. Jack, who realised that their hired car was not up to the task of carting supplies up that mountain, came up with a proposal for Don Giovanni.

"Signore", he said, "we paid a substantial deposit on our hired vehicle, but that car is of no good use to us whilst we make the house up at Valparaiso Vecchio liveable. It would be of great help to us if we can use your truck for a while to get building materials up there with you taking over the lease and use our car for that time. Of course we pay you and we can negotiate the price".

The Don wasn't sure about taking over the lease and would have to think about it. But for the time being, they could have the truck under the condition that when the Don had to do a delivery, he could still use his truck. It was agreed. The fact that Jack and Susan ordered a substantial amount of supplies for their new home from the Don's building supplies business straight away, probably helped the deal along.

Susan was over the moon about how the day had developed and immediately wanted to go and buy all new furniture and a good bed. Jack had to slow her down a bit, tomorrow was another day, and they had much more choice in the harbour town. The Don fully agreed with that decision, and there was a reason for that, as Jack and Susan would find out later.

Don Giovanni and the owner of the local furniture shop, a signor Bartolomeo, in Novo Valparaiso, did not like each other at all. This was also because they were members of opposite political parties. Some of the older generation were communists, especially out in the country, as were half of Italy's people after the war. Mr Bartolomeo was still a staunch communist.

As it turned out, Susan had to put her shopping spree on hold because the next day they found the group deeply sad with some of them in tears. Monti had died that night and the boys did not know what to do next. The friends had been taking turns sitting with the sick Monti for most of the night, but Monti had given up. He had never stopped talking about the two children, blaming himself for their deaths. "What now Jack? How can we give him a dignified burial? How can I tell his parents?" Paul asked with desperation in his voice. "We can hardly go and dig a grave in the paddock!" Jack, trying to calm him, said, "Listen, all of you, We work something out, and Paul, you must go to work as normal."

Jack and Susan discussed the dilemma and concluded that it would be best if the body was returned to the sea. That way, when his body was found, he would be seen as one of the many refugees who perished at sea, and he would get a decent burial.

That evening, they drove to the shed and discussed their proposal with the group. It was not an easy decision, but they saw no other solution. After everyone had said their final goodbyes, only Paul and Samson would go with Jack and Susan for the burial, as this had to be done quickly and quietly. Monti's body was carefully rolled into the bedsheets and gently transferred to their truck.

The four then drove to the harbour city. They kept going along the shore until they found a desolate and suitable spot where they put the body as far as possible into the surf and rolled the body out of the sheets and into the sea.

The four of them stood together silently and watched the waves take hold of the body till soon it was out of sight.

Deeply sad, they hardly spoke on the way back. Only Samson said, as he was fighting back tears, that Monti was a hero and that he had deserved so much better. Susan replied that together, they would find a way to build a memorial to Monti, so his bravery would always be remembered.

Chapter Twelve

Chapter Twelve

Don Giovani came to their hotel the next morning and ordered a bottle of Chianti with his coffee, for which he never paid. He had news, but first, he emphasised that Valparaiso Vecchio would be a great buy with its beautiful views, the vineyard on the slope and the healthy air to breathe. "Now you sound like a real salesman, and hopefully, this won't affect the price too much," Jack remarked. "I don't have a final price yet", the Don said. "But there are thirteen houses in the village instead of ten, and all the owners want their share."

"Well," Jack said, "I never knew that houses in Italy had babies overnight. We counted only nine plus the bigger house. Anyway, we'll drive up and count again", and with a wink, he continued, "I can assure you that we can count to ten Signor". Then, changing the subject, Jack asked the Don if he knew how people used to get water to the village.

"I must confess I don't know", the Don replied, shrugging his shoulders. As far as he knew, they always had water. They probably collected rainwater, was his guess. "When we were up there, we didn't see any water tanks or anything", Jack said. "But we will go and have another look today and come by your yard on our way up there to get a few things".

Paul had offered to go with them the next time Jack and Susan went up to the mountain village again, so they picked him up and then went to the Don's sale yard. They loaded a lot of straw and other things onto the truck and then went up the road. Because Jack had been telling Paul about the possible water problem, Paul kept his eyes open and intently scrutinised the landscape. He asked Jack to stop the truck after they had driven more than halfway up. They were on one of the big sweeping bends in the road. "You talked about the water supply", Paul said, "If you look over there, it looks like there is a little stream coming from the mountain".

After parking the truck on the side of the road, they went to investigate, and yes, there was a stream. It was small but quite strong, with good fresh water. They got back in the truck and continued up the road. When they arrived at the terraced track leading up to the village, Jack very carefully manoeuvred the truck up the steps, which were only about 3 to 4 inches high, and about four to five feet deep.

After they managed to get up there and Paul saw the village, he enthusiastically exclaimed, "Oh wow!!! Are you guys really going to buy all this?" Jack replied, "If we can, yes, but let's first unload the truck and then have a good look around." There were only nine houses in addition to the main house, as Jack had counted before, but three of them had a small shed in the back. "I think they may be trying to count those tiny outhouses as houses, but I hope not," Jack said.

Whilst the two men were counting the houses, Susan did a thorough tour of the 'big house'. In one of the rooms, she found an old-fashioned prayer stool. It was made of nicely carved wood. It had a shelf or top on it, almost like a writing desk, a drawer underneath. When she managed to get the drawer open, she found a manuscript in beautiful handwriting. Susan couldn't read it as it was in what appeared to be Latin. She showed it to Jack and Paul when they came back. Jack said that they would have a look at that when they got back to their hotel later. Paul had to go to work and needed a lift, and Jack wanted to go to the hardware store and see Don Giovanni about a pump for getting water to the village.

Jack and Susan dropped Paul off at the bistro before going to the hardware store. The Don was there, and Jack asked him if he had any knowledge about a 'click clack' pump that uses no fuel or electricity but works with the water pressure. No, the Don had never heard about such a thing, but if Jack wanted one, he would enquire. "Yes", Jack said, "we want a pump like that and a big plastic water tank of a couple of thousand gallons, and please, can we have this as soon as possible."

After taking the order, the Don asked if they had counted the houses at Valparaiso Vecchio. "Sure did", Jack answered. "There are definitely only ten houses in total, but many of them are hardly worth that name". Looking puzzled, the Don said, "But then why is it that more people have put in a claim?" Jack replied, "All I can think of is that they are trying to sell the sheds or outhouses, which are at the back of three houses, as houses but nobody can call any of those a house. No, too many people have dollar signs in their eyes now there is a serious buyer for the village."

"We will sort it out", the Don said, "and by the way, Signor Bartolomeo ordered a lot of fencing material, and I think it is for the meadow above Valparaiso Vecchio". Puzzled, Jack responded, "We have no intentions of starting a cattle farm; we are just after a quiet pensioner life".

After Susan finished shopping for water containers, brooms and buckets, among other things, from Don's shop, they picked up three of the boys on their way back up the mountain track and brought them to Valparaiso Vecchio. Addo, Joshua and Perry were the lucky first three, and they were over the moon. They couldn't believe their luck as each could choose their own house to fix up. For the time being, they would sleep in the big house. They promised that they would work hard to make all the other houses liveable. "Be very careful and do not take chances on the roofs. We can't have any of you getting an accident. And watch out, as the neighbours are building a fence up there; don't let them see you", were their instructions.

That evening, Jack and Susan studied the manuscript that Susan had found in the big house, but they could make neither head nor tail out of the writings. "Let's go to the harbour town tomorrow", Susan said, "We need to buy groceries for the boys again anyway, and then we can also look for a bed and furniture. We can ask at the cathedral if someone can help us translate this document."

Chapter Thirteen

The next day, Jack and Susan drove to the big harbour town again but were disappointed by the answer they received at the cathedral. They were told that nobody would have the time. "Yes, we do speak Latin, modern Latin, but this is an old language, and we have no time or resources to do the translation". Susan asked them if they knew anyone else who could help them, and they suggested the museum or the University.

At the museum, the reception was much friendlier, and they were happy to help. They found the document interesting. "We will not have the time to work constantly on this, but we will keep you up to date," they said, and all they were asking for in return was that they could keep the document for their museum after they were done. Jack and Susan both agreed.

They spent the rest of the day shopping and found out that there were several shops with good second-hand furniture and other goods, and it was so much cheaper than buying new ones. They had a truck full by the time they left for home. When they drove up to the village the next day, they were surprised by what those three boys had done already, enabling them to bring the rest of the friends up.

Now, all nine friends were living at Valparaiso Vecchio. Paul was still working at the restaurant down in the village below. The rest of them had been working on the track to their mountain village to make it more accessible. In order to not draw attention to their presence, that work had to be stopped because Signor Bartolomeo's men were erecting a fence around the whole meadow above Old Valparaiso. Jack and Susan told the group to keep a low profile and always keep an eye out for any other people coming up the mountain. They knew, however, that this could not be maintained, not in the long term, and decided to take the mayor, Don Giovanni, in their confidence. They invited the Don for a farewell lunch at their hotel. Jack and Susan made sure that the Don was served well and was completely satisfied. Boy, could that man eat and drink. Then Jack started to turn the conversation to the subject he had intended to talk about with the Don.

"Signor Giovanni", he said, "we have a big favour to ask you, and we hope that you can help us". He told the Don that when they left Africa, their workers, who lost the jobs they loved with no prospect of finding another similar situation, were very sad and asked if they could come with them and that they had promised them, if the circumstances became favourable, they would try and get them over.

"Now that we have committed ourselves to buying Valparaiso Vecchio and there is a lot of work to do, we really could use our men now", Jack said. "We know that the immigration laws are very strict in this country", he continued, but my wife and I need help, and these men would love to come and work for us again. We don't want any trouble for you, but is it possible to get temporary visas or work permits or something like that for them? In the meantime, we can work on getting their paperwork in order for a more permanent situation. Again, we don't want to get anybody in trouble, but if we wait for the bureaucracy to have the paperwork ready, we will be too old for all this." The Don said that it was a very complex situation, but that he would see what could be done. "Right now, though, we do have a more intimidating and local problem", he said. "There have been objections against your click-clack pump and pipework as well as accusations that you are stealing water from our town". A little irritated, Jack replied, "Well, sir, what I would suggest is that you and some of the main protesters come with me and I'll show them how this pump works. From the forty litres that come through the pump, only two litres go to our village. I don't know where this comes from, but surely nobody can miss that little bit of water we use. It is all in the documentation that came with the pump."

"I must confess that I have not read that paperwork," said the Don. "Never mind, we all know where the complaints come from, but I will talk to them and keep you informed", he continued. "Thank you, Signor", Jack said and turning the conversation back to the boy's permits, he asked the Don about it again. "Oh yes, about your workers. Well, full immigration permits are nearly impossible in Italy at the moment. I'll try to get work permits for them. That may work if I tell them that you bought an old local farm and are investing a lot of money here." Jack said, "That's what we're doing". But farming? He had no desire to start another farm.

Chapter Fourteen

An excited young Ben came to see Jack, "Boss!" he shouted out. "I had a look at the meadow up there. There is an inclination in the ground in a straight line to the fence above our village!" Jack placed his hand on Ben's shoulder and said, "Hmmm, that's interesting, Ben. The fence workers have packed up, so when they're gone, we are going to have a look." When the coast was clear, Jack climbed up with Benjamin and Levy to take a closer look at the area that Benjamin had indicated, and yes, there certainly was an incline straight over the paddock towards them. "Well spotted, Ben", Jack said.

The ground was levelled but only for the last few metres to the fence. This looked strange. Levy said, "If you ask me, there was a canal or something to bring water to our village, and they must have blocked it for the last few metres." "Yes", said Jack, convinced that Levy was right.

The next afternoon, Jack noticed that Bartolomeo's fence workers had hung up signs against trespassing on private property. After studying the situation and discussing this with Benjamin and Levy, Jack decided that they could drill from outside the fence and see if there was water a few metres further. He purchased a hand drill from The Don's hardware store, and they started drilling towards the end of the day.

To drill horizontally into a slope was not easy, but, after they had excavated a kind of platform, it became more straightforward. However, they encountered other problems. The trench or canal was filled with stones, which made it very hard work. The handle of the drill was too short to go far enough, so because Jack did not allow the young men to climb the fence and trespass, they lengthened the handle of the drill. After a few more days of hard work, some water came through, then a bit more. This looked hopeful, and Jack went to buy a whole bunch of plastic pipework from the hardware store. When he pushed a pipe up the drilled hole to see if clear water would run out, and it did, the pipes were connected to the water tank. To everyone's delight, it all worked beautifully. The next job was to connect the tank to the village houses. Everyone had learned new skills in the process, and Susan was over the moon when she received running water in her house.

The next time Jack went to town to pick up the mail, there was a summons from a law firm. Signor Bartolomeo accused them of trespassing and stealing his water. Jack went to the Don with the letter and showed it to him. "You will have to get a lawyer for this," he said. "Can you recommend one?" Jack asked. "I would go and find one in the harbour town," the Don said, "I am not sure if the only one here in town would be impartial." After asking around in the big harbour town, he found two suitable lawyers. One had already been engaged by Mr Bartolomeo, so that left Mr Marco Carnivale, the more expensive of the two, but Jack did have confidence in this lawyer.

Looking at the photos Jack had taken of the part outside the fence, Marco asked, "You guys did not go inside the fence?" Jack responded, "No, we did not, and I can swear by that." "Strange",

Marco said. "It looks like there was water going to Valparaiso all the time, but someone blocked it." Jack nodded. "Yes, that's what it looks like," he said. He had a court case on his hands, and it was probably going to cost a lot of time and money.

However, Susan wanted her big windows, so on his way back to Valparaiso, Jack went to see Don Giovanni at the sales yards and ordered six big windows for the main house to surprise Susan so she could have her view. The Don's advice was to make it double glazing as in winter, the wind came right from that quarter and was very cold. Jack thought, "more money", but he agreed, and with winter approaching, he was keen to get the double-glazed windows installed in time. He asked the Don if he had any idea when the windows would be arriving. "I'll chase it up for you", the Don answered. "But they have to come from a great distance. They are not made locally, but I certainly hope you will get them installed before the winter cold sets in. May I also recommend that you load the truck with firewood?" With a wink, Jack responded, "You may, as long as it's not as expensive as my windows."

"If I may be of further advice," the Don continued." "You also need to start thinking about pruning the grapevines now and save the branches to use in your fireplace. Do you know what to do?" Jack shrugged his shoulders and said, "I have no idea, really. We had no grapevines in our part of Africa. Maybe I should go and visit another vineyard to learn about it?" The Don responded that it could be useful to do that and that he would see what he could arrange for Jack.

"I can give you this tip to start you off", Don said, and he explained to Jack, that when pruning the vines, to always leave the main trunk intact and train the vine to let it grow in the desired direction. All the long and new branches should be cut from two knots of the stem, and at the beginning of spring, the earth around the vines must be turned over and manure or other suitable fertiliser mixed in the soil. "That's it in broad lines", the Don continued, and, always being the salesman, he added, "You'll need clippers. Have you got any?" With a little sarcasm, Jack responded, "Thank you very much, Signor, and here I was thinking that we had retired when we sold our farm." Then he smiled and said, "But seriously, your help and advice with everything is very much appreciated," and with a wink, he continued, "I'll get the firewood and ten pairs of clippers from your store".

Chapter Fifteen

Susan received a fat letter from the museum, and when she read through the document, there was something very interesting. It stated that three of the dwellings in Old Valparaiso had built little sheds or rooms onto their house. One to keep a cow in for the winter, one to store fodder, and one for their worker to sleep in so that he did not have to walk up to the village every day.

Jack took the translation to the Don and told him that this was proof that those three outhouses belonged to the main houses and were not individual dwellings. The Don agreed and said that he would contact those people and see if he could get the final figures round. "Some of our villagers will not be very happy", he said. "Well," Jack responded, "They should not have put in false claims; they took the risk." The Don agreed, "That's right," he said and then asked how Jack was getting on with the court case.

"Very slowly", Jack answered. "As everything always is where bureaucracy is involved. Hopefully, my lawyer will bring this case to a good outcome before too long." The Don nodded sympathetically and said, "Well, I have some good news for you. Your men have been approved, and I can now give you a piece of paper stating that they can come and temporarily work on your farm. I did have to specifically state that they will be working on your 'farm', in order to get the permits".

Jack was very relieved that this was arranged so quickly. He expected the process to take a lot longer as, in his experience, bureaucracy takes its time. With a smile, he said, "That's great news, Signor; thank you very much for your help! My men will be so happy, and I can now make arrangements to get them over to Valparaiso as soon as possible, and the work can start!"

Soon, it was all hands on deck or, rather, in the vineyard, and it was hard work. The vineyard was laid out as terraces around the mountain slope, and the boys had to walk all the way back to go up or down. However, with nine pairs of extra hands, the work was accomplished before too long and before winter set in, and it did so with a vengeance.

It was bitterly cold in their village halfway up the mountain. Soon, there wasn't sufficient firewood, and Jack, Susan and the young men had to economise. At least there was wood for the fireplace in the kitchen of the big house after Jack had bought another load of firewood. Susan was still able to cook for everybody. This was a daily big job because, boy, those young guys could eat!

Revel and Aron stayed in one of the small houses that had an old-fashioned bread oven, and they became the bakers of the village. However, the wood shortage warranted only one baking session a week. "We'll make sure to stockpile firewood for the next winter", Jack said.

For now, the young men bunked together at night in some of the little houses because not all the roofs on all the houses had been repaired yet. There weren't enough roof tiles to finish them all, and Don couldn't get any more second-hand ones. New red roof tiles were available but were very expensive. Someone remarked that half the church roof was also repaired with red tiles, but Jack did not want to get the tiles from the church roof right now. He reckoned it was too cold for repairing roofs anyway, and there was another big problem that had priority.

The water pipes froze, and some even burst. This had to be fixed immediately. They had learned the hard way that water pipes in European climates needed to be at least a foot under the ground for protection against frost. For now, they bound whatever straw and any other material they could spare around the pipes. Where possible, they dug trenches and put pipes underground. At long last, Susan had water in her house again, but they all realised that before the next winter, they would have a big job on their hands to fix the issue properly and permanently.

Usually, after dinner and before retiring to their own quarters, the whole group stayed with Jack and Susan in the big house the whole evening because it was warm and cosy there. The boys would often sing some of their old home songs. One evening, Susan asked Jack to get his clarinet out of the mothballs and play for them. It didn't sound very skilled but the rhythm was surely present. Susan, being the music teacher she was, saw potential.

Chapter Sixteen

The next time they were in the harbour town, Susan went back to the second-hand shop where she had seen some musical instruments. She bought a guitar and a trumpet. When she brought the instruments home, they all wanted to give it a try. It soon was obvious that Addo had the most talent for the guitar and Aron for the trumpet. Levy could play the guitar, too, but Addo definitely stood out. Under the gentle supervision of music teacher Susan, they became better and better.

From then on, and almost habitually, they played music and sang together every evening. Benjamin would always drum the rhythm by using his hands on the edge of the table, and Susan decided that he needed a drum set, so when Jack and Susan went to the harbour town again, they took young Benjamin with them, and he was in for a big surprise. Susan asked the owner of the second-hand music shop if he would allow Ben to have a go at the drum set that was for sale. "Of course, no problem", the man said. He even helped and instructed Ben on what was what and how to go about it.

It was clear that Ben had it in him to play this instrument, just as Susan had thought. He was over the moon with his present and promised to practise hard on it. "Very well, but not in our house, young man. You pick your own; plenty to choose from", Jack said with a wink.

Before they headed back home, Susan went to the museum again and collected the next bundle of translations from their manuscript. She started to read it in the car, but it was some days later when she told Jack what she had read.

"Jack", she said, "You should hear this," and then she told him that as far as she understood it, the latest translations of the manuscript she picked up from the museum stated that the meadow above Valparaiso Alto belonged to their village and not to Bartolomeo! "Wow!" Jack said excitedly, "This means that the water is ours as we always thought. It also means we may be able to keep some animals as well".

Immediately Jack rushed off to the Don, and showed him the document. Patting Jack on the shoulder the Don said, "You must go to your lawyer immediately, my friend. This will give a whole new spin on your court case. I am very glad for you!" Jack made an appointment straight away and went back to the big harbour town to see Marco Carnivale, his lawyer.

"That is very interesting, Signor", the lawyer said, "Now we can get some money out of Signor Bartolomeo. I will try to get a hearing in court as soon as possible. We'll get the person who translated the manuscript as a witness." Jack said that he would go to the museum and ask. He was sure the gentleman wouldn't mind testifying for them. "But, please, all I want you to do is get your fees, and the court costs out of this. That's all my wife, and I want". Marco was quite surprised and responded, "OK, if that's your wish, but we could ask for a lot more". Jack said, "No, thank you. Just see that you get all the costs covered, will you?"

In court, Mr Bartolomeo had brought some of his cronies along, and they were very loudly making a nuisance of themselves. After two warnings, the judge had the lot removed from his Court. It didn't take long before he fully agreed with the accused and said to dismiss Bartolomeo's claim. After loud complaints by Mr Bartolomeo about this ruling, Jack's lawyer declared that he had strict instructions from his client only to ask the judge for cost compensation and nothing more.

Even so, in the next issue of his little local newspaper, Signor Bartolomeo wrote a nasty piece about foreigners who stole the local farms and so on. The Don and Jack counteracted by placing an article in the other local paper about what actually happened and that some locals had unlawfully grabbed things that did not belong to them, then took innocent people to court accusing them of trespassing and stealing water when it was the accusers who did the trespassing and the stealing. But justice had prevailed, and the accusers were ordered to pay all the costs.

With the legal matters behind him, Jack was able to focus on Valparaiso Vecchio again. There were a number of things that needed to be sorted, and when spring came to the country, it was glorious. However, at Valparaiso Vecchio, everyone was too busy to just enjoy the beautiful weather. Jack split up his workforce into three parts: one group to work in the vineyard, one to fix all the plumbing work and one to take care of the firewood.

The plumbing group was doing an excellent job supplying every house with its own water as well as the pond with the fountain on the village square, which had been cleaned out and was now waiting for some fish. Jack also made sure that the people in Valparaiso Novo always received sufficient water from the stream so that everyone would be satisfied.

The group responsible for the next winter's firewood supply discovered this was easier said than done. Don Giovanni, having become a good friend, came to the rescue again. He told them where the locals were getting their firewood.

On the mountain on top was a state forest, and the rangers would mark trees that could be harvested. The locals were allowed to cut those trees in such a way that they did not damage many nearby trees. The Don didn't mind at all telling them. After all, he made more money on chains, chainsaws and other equipment necessary for all this than he did on selling firewood himself.

Getting the wood was hard work. Cutting down a tree was the easy bit. To get the huge logs out and not destroy too much of the rest of the forest was another matter. Essentially, the logs had to be cut up and moved by hand until they reached where the four-wheel truck could be loaded and then bring the wood home. Jack promised himself and the team that he would soon have a winch system fitted to the truck, to help move the logs in the future.

Of course, with this exercise, Jack's workers became more exposed to the locals, which, again, prompted a series of articles in the local newspaper. This, in turn, resulted in reactions from the opposite paper stating that the people who had bought Old Valparaiso were allowed to bring their own workers to the farm under certain conditions, which were all complied with.

Chapter Seventeen

It wasn't until summer that Susan finally got her double-glazed bay windows. Installing them was a time-consuming, tricky job to make them fit, but the result was worth it. The large windows exposed breathtaking views over the vineyard whilst letting in an abundance of natural light, making the house feel bright and airy inside. The windows and the views they showed off, were admired by all, and Susan was very happy.

At the end of summer, all the grapes were ripe and had to be harvested. Jack had purchased a small hand wine press, and with instructions from the Don they proceeded to make their own wine. The empty water containers were now of good use. They had collected a lot of empty bottles, mainly via Paul from the bistro, where he was still working.

The whole group became involved in the process, and they thought it was great fun when it came to crushing the grapes. Ozie, who often stayed the weekend to be with Paul, had offered to help with the crushing. They all thought this was fantastic and encouraged her to lift her skirt up high as others brought more grapes to the drum, thereby gaining a glimpse of her shapely legs.

The grapes were very sweet and very dark, and the young men joked that colour did not matter to them whilst they were crushing them. Susan was delighted when they all started to sing and even more so when she discovered that Ozie had a beautiful voice which harmonised perfectly with the voices of the boys.

The sweetness of grapes depends on the amount of sunshine they get in a particular year. This year, they had sufficient sunshine, and the taste of the wine would become fantastic, not unlike Madeira wine, a fortified wine, according to the experts. The wine harvest was not very big this year, only about a hundred bottles, as only the vines that had been pruned had lots of fruit. Nevertheless, a label had to be designed. Together, they discussed a name for their wine. They voted, and the label became 'Monti Alto Wines', after their friend Monti.

Someone mentioned that the village should also be named after him. Everyone agreed, as not only did they all find the name Valparaiso Vecchio a mouthful and difficult to pronounce, but they also wanted to commemorate their friend, a hero who gave his life in his attempt to save others. And so it was agreed. Both, the wine label and the village, would be known as 'Monti Alto'.

When Jack saw the Don again, he spoke to him about the renaming of the old village. The Don thought it would be a very good idea to name the wine and the village with the same name. He said, "Valparaiso never had a postcode anyway". Don was confident that the 'Poste Italiane' would approve of it. "Except maybe the postman," he laughed, "They may not like to climb the hill for every letter". "That's not a problem. I'll pick up our mail myself. We come down here every day anyway", Jack said. "Ok", the Don responded, "As the mayor, I will start the process of changing the name officially".

When it was time again for the pruning of the grapevines, they managed to complete another two and a half of the terraces. Jack said, "Next year, we'll have it all done".

Whilst the harvest was still small, storage of the wine was possible in the small cellars of two of the houses. Jack knew he would have to extend one or both cellars when the harvests would get bigger each year. The vineyard would become a small winery. Later, Jack often said to visitors who were buying their product, that a small winery was better than a big farm and that he would know as he used to have one.

Chapter Eighteen

When Susan received the next translation of their manuscript, it was, again, exciting news. It revealed that whilst the church was being built, a young chaplain had taken up residence in the big house to offer services and other activities. When, at long last, the work was finished, the church had to be consecrated.

That could only be done by the bishop. The village, and therefore the church, was not easily accessible and certainly not by car, as the bishop found out when his vehicle stopped a good hundred metres short of the church.

The whole village population was dressed in their Sunday best, and all the dignitaries from the neighbourhood were present. The bishop, his one hundred and fifty-kilo frame clad in full apparel, stepped out of the limousine and started to walk up the steps. But only halfway up, the poor man collapsed and had a heart attack. He was taken to hospital, where he died a short time later. The little church had not been consecrated. "It was never officially a church, and it means we can freely use it," Jack said. This was an interesting new point of view.

"Come", he said, taking Susan by the hand, "let's go and have a look". They entered the church through the side door and found the key to the front doors. Like many of the other houses, the roof of the church was also leaking, and that had done much damage. Some of the pews were still intact, but others were only good for firewood, and there was not much else of interest left.

From several dilapidated houses in other villages, the Don said that he would be able to get hold of a good set of slate tiles to repair the church roof. That was a big job as the roof was higher and steeper than those of the houses, and nobody had the experience to work with slate, but The Don helped them out once more. He knew a good roof tiler, and, with his help, the church roof was soon restored whilst gaining enough red tiles in the process to finish the roofs of the remaining unfinished houses.

After the church roof was repaired, Susan went inside and sang a few notes to find out what the acoustics inside the building would be like. They were very good. Susan thought that this was because of the hard stone masonry of the walls and floors, and she wondered how those men in the past knew how to build to achieve such great acoustics. She decided there and then that from now on, the music lessons would no longer be done in the house but in the church. Susan expected the music and voices would sound so much better in the church, and they did.

One day, Ozie introduced her friend Rosie to everyone in the mountain village. Ozie met her some time ago at the markets where they often went in the early mornings, and as they're both from the same part of Africa, they soon started to talk and became friends. On one occasion, Rosie asked her new friend what she was doing on weekends when she was free. Ozie said, "What do you mean? I have every weekend off, don't you?" Rosie told her that she only gets every second weekend off. "Every other weekend, I have to accompany the madam and her children to church", she said, pulling a face, "And I do not like it because I don't understand anything that happens in that church".

Ozie sympathised with her new friend and told her that she had a boyfriend and spent most weekends with him at a village up the mountain now called Monti Alto. "Did you know that there are nine boys from our country?" She asked. "No", Rosie answered, "I heard some rumours but have only seen one at the little bistro." "Ah, that is my Paul, but there are eight more great guys in the village. Come with me next time." Rosie did, and she fitted right in. She was welcomed and became a regular visitor, and it soon became apparent that she was very musical and had a beautiful singing voice. She sang with a raspy voice just like some well-known international singers of Negro Spirituals. She soon formed a duo with Levy.

Rosie was very impressed and loved that each boy had his own house. Levy fell for her very quickly, and during many hours of practising their song, laughing together and reminiscing about their home country, Rosie soon fell in love with Levy, too. "If this continues, we will get an African settlement in Italy in no time", Jack said with a wink.

As always, it was very cosy in the big house that winter. Even now, despite most of the other houses having their own stove, the young people still liked to come together for Susan's cooking and to sing together. Susan had bought a whole bunch of music. Most of it was Negro Spirituals and jazz. This was a great success with the boys and girls. They could copy and sing along and even made their own interpretations. There were sufficient musical instruments available, as Susan had been buying more in town. The group was getting better and better under the guidance of their music teacher. Some could even play the half notes that people from Africa could do so well and which had made jazz so famous all over the world.

Chapter Nineteen

At the dinner table of the Bartolomeo family's household, there was the usual talk about 'all the bloody immigrants' and 'dirty refugees', who, according to the father, 'spoiled the local labour market', and so on. Signora Bartolomeo had long given up arguing with her husband, and so, today, too, she kept quiet even if she did not agree with him.

Signor Bartolomeo's youngest son Mario had autism, but he understood much more from what was said than what anybody realised or gave him credit for. The boy had little support at home, was mainly on his own and had hardly been to school. Mario was a big boy. His greatest passion was eating, and he liked watching his father's goats up the mountain meadow. Every day, he could be seen going up there with his shepherd's staff in his hand.

Signor Bartolomeo often harped on about the foreigners 'who had taken our land and much of our water', repeating his same old story. Today he had discovered something new. It clearly angered him that the people who lived up the mountain had installed six big, double-glazed windows to enjoy the view. "Can you imagine the waste!?" he ranted.

Mario had listened with full attention, and a plan came up in his head that evening after he went to bed. He knew what to do to help his father. Having looked after the goats up the mountain meadow for several summers, he knew all the paths around that area. One evening, after dark, he would go up the mountain and smash all those big windows of the houses where those 'bad people' lived, and he did.

So, on a warm evening, Mario sneaked quietly out of the house. Armed with his shepherd staff, he went up to the village on the mountain. The staff, made of tough wood, was a pole of about seven feet long and commonly used by the mountain shepherds. In the right hands, it certainly could be a formidable weapon. Slowly, Mario walked around the little mountain village until he came to the side of the vineyard, and then he sneaked up to the big house.

As it happened, on that warm night, Levy did what he would often do when it was too hot to sleep inside. He went on the roof of the lean-to to his house to try and sleep there, but he wasn't comfortable there either and couldn't get to sleep. Levy was looking at the stars when, suddenly, he saw a staff passing by. He slipped from the roof and followed the intruder, who went up to Jack and Susan's place.

When Mario took a big swing with his staff to smash a window, Levy gave him a smack against his head. The staff rattled against the window without doing any damage, but fortunately for Mario, this woke Jack, who came to investigate immediately. Levy kept on hitting Mario until he screamed, but Jack stopped the onslaught. Levy was very upset, "He was trying to break the misses' beautiful windows!"

"Let's see who we got here," said Jack. They made some light and brought the boy in. "Well, well, if that is not young Mario Bartolomeo, what do you have to say for yourself, young man?"

The boy said nothing but was feeling his face as if to make sure something was left of it. One eye was closed, and he had a bloody nose. In that state, Jack couldn't let him go home by himself, so he put him in the truck and went to drop him off at his home. He didn't think they would ever see Mario again up here after having taken a beating like that.

Signora Bartolomeo had checked on her son before bed and was hysterical that he was not in his bed. Her husband, oblivious to the situation, was sleeping, but she couldn't. Then she heard the truck. "Where have you been? What has happened to you, oh my baby!", she cried. After some prompting, the boy confessed to his mother what he had done, or rather had intended to do. "I wanted to help my papà, but a black devil stood guard and beat me up. I did not have a chance", he moaned. "Oh, my poor baby, better not tell your father that! Tell him that you went for a walk because you couldn't sleep and got hurt because you stepped on a rake!"

Mario did that the next day, but his father did not believe one syllable of his story and was pretty sure that something else had happened.

After Jack told the Don the story, the Don said that he wanted to put the story in the newspaper. Jack disagreed. "Look", he said, "The boy has autism, but he is okay, and he has learned a lesson, let's leave it at that."

However, one way or another, Signor Bartolomeo found out what happened to his son. As a result, he started another campaign in his newspaper about illegal immigrants and refugees. This action presented Jack and Mayor Giovanni with a problem not so easily dealt with.

Chapter Twenty

Susan returned to the second-hand music shop, looking for a trombone and a double bass. She talked to the shopkeeper about the instruments she wanted to buy. "Yes, I can help you with a double bass", the shopkeeper said. "The strings will need replacing", but it's in great condition otherwise".

Unfortunately, he didn't have a trombone at the moment, but he certainly would look out for one.

"Maybe I can help you to get a trombone," said a gentleman who stood nearby. Then he asked, "Do I hear an English accent? "I am David Kronenberg, by the way." Susan introduced herself and asked if he was the famous conductor, David Kronenberg. "Yes, although not famous over here quite yet," the conductor answered and with a smile, he continued, "But I am doing my best to teach the Italian people that there is great music other than opera. May I ask what your purpose is for those instruments?"

"Mmm, that is a long story", answered Susan. "In that case, may I invite you to come and sit down for a coffee so you can tell me your story?" David asked. "My husband is waiting," Susan answered, "if you don't mind that he comes too, then yes, that'll be great". "But, of course," said David.

They went to meet Jack, and Susan introduced the two men to each other. "Please call me David", the conductor said, and the three went off to his very nice hotel for coffee. Jack, who was a little unsure about this handsome fellow who seemed so friendly with his wife, soon relaxed as Susan explained that David was a famous conductor and international music expert. They told David where they were from and that they had bought a village in the mountains. David, in turn, told them that he was from Vienna in Austria. His parents had immigrated to the US shortly after he was born. Music was in their blood. Susan said that she was a music teacher and had a group of poor students she was teaching. "I see. so, are you buying these instruments for your students?" David asked while he beckoned the waiter to order a second round of coffee. Susan told him about the group of friends, now living with them in their village and what they had been through trying to find a better life for themselves. "They love to sing and play music and are so natural at it", she added. Jack leaned over to David and said quietly, "My wife is a little timid and shy about her work with those boys, but with her helping them study and practise, they are becoming quite good". "Well", Susan said with a bashful smile. "In winter, one cannot do much else halfway up the mountain. It gets so cold up there sometimes. that you long for Africa".

"I am on a short break right now" David said, "and I have a few days available. I would love to come and visit your 'Monti Alto'". Jack looked at Susan, who nodded, and he then responded, "Sir, how could we refuse? We are driving up there as soon as my wife has finished her shopping. You are welcome to tag along." "Great!" said David, "I'll go and get my car and wait here for you".

"Oh no", Susan said, slightly panicked as she realised they didn't have anywhere for visitors to stay as yet. "I have nothing decent to eat, and where is David going to sleep?!" Jack laughed and said with a wink, "he will eat what we all eat, and he can stay in the lovely little hotel where we stayed".

And so it happened that a luxury Mercedes followed the old truck up to the mountain track. It was slow going after the rain today, and they were back later than expected. Two women, who were employed as cooks to help Susan with the cooking, had already begun to prepare the evening meal, but everyone was waiting for Jack and Susan to return.

The boys and Ozie had begun to practise while waiting for dinner time. They played their instruments and sang songs from their homeland. When they arrived, Susan took David to the church first. The band was in great form, and David, quite flabbergasted, went quiet for a while, but then he said enthusiastically, "That was fantastic! You guys could go far with this group." "Thank you", Susan said. "Yes, these young people are quite talented. We haven't been practising very long, and they already sound great! But for now, whilst Jack shows you around in our little village, I'll see about dinner".

Meanwhile, the cooks had done a good job with what was available to them to prepare a meal and within a short while, dinner was on the table. There was not much conversation during dinner, as this was the first time they had a stranger as a guest. Susan apologised for the simple meal, but David said, "It was a delicious meal, thank you, and compliments to your wonderful cooks. Maybe it is the healthy mountain air because I have not eaten so much for a long time".

After dinner, Jack and Susan took their guest to sit in front of their beautiful view to sample their own wines. David was all geared up and said, "You should come to Milano. We can make you great all over the world. I will give you a manager/agent who is extraordinarily good. I trust him completely. If you agree, the sky's the limit", he raved enthusiastically. It was hard to get a word in, but when Jack finally did, he said, "David, it all sounds fantastic for the boys. But you don't know a very important detail, and that is that these young men are stateless, and by the law of the land, they can be returned to their homeland any day."

"Dear people, no need to have any worries about that. I happen to have connections and can fix that problem", said David reassuringly. "Really? Can you do that? I would be endlessly happy if you could organise that", Susan said excitedly, and Jack said, "Yes, that would be fantastic and solve a lot of problems. It would be a godsend, but how do you foresee this all happening?" David replied, "I will send someone here to get all the names and information of the young men and Ozie as well. She is a great singer."

"Oh, but you haven't heard Rosie yet. She is special too with her deep, raspy voice," said Susan. "I can't wait to hear her, too", David said. "You guys can go very far with this group. Does the band have a name? We will advertise and promote them". Susan said, "Yes, I think they want to call themselves 'The Monti Alto Group', after their friend. I hope you will agree with that?" David nodded, "An unusual name, but we'll get used to that. I see them going to Hollywood already."

"Please go slowly with them", Susan said with a worried look on her face, "They have hardly been exposed to that world". Jack added, "Your plans will have initial and substantial costs; how do you see that taken care of?" David again reassured them. "We don't need to worry about the cost right now", he said, "We will draw up a contract in which you continue to be their guardians, and I provide the finances and a manager. When they become famous, they can pay me back. But you're right, we must not make the young friends feel intimidated by it all. They will play best when they are at ease".

Chapter Twenty-One

A few days after David had gone, a car with two gentlemen drove up. One of them was very tall and skinny, the other quite short and fat. A bigger difference would not be possible. The tall one was quick and energetic, while the short one was slow but very observant.

They introduced themselves to Jack and Susan as Saly Lackerheim, impresario and agent. He was the tall one, and Signor Da Contimari, the short one, was a public servant from the Department of Foreign Affairs. Saly went with Susan to discuss the group and his short-term plans for them. At the same time, Signor Da Contimari wanted the boys and girls, one by one, in the church. He had a stack of paperwork with him and a camera to take some photographs of each applicant. That took the rest of the day. Jack acted as an interpreter in half English and half Italian. It became a long process.

Towards three o'clock in the afternoon, Signor Da Contimari had finished and was ready to go, but Saly wanted to stay. "Mille grazie signore, no problem", he said. "I'll stay a little longer to hear the young men play and return later." That evening Saly was treated to a performance from their home repertoire.

"That is pretty good, especially that slow jazz," said the agent. "Please play now one of your favourites, something you guys really like." Aron put the trumpet to his lips and started 'When The Saints Go Marching In'. Jack joined in with the clarinet and then, Benjamin on the drums, followed by Addo on the guitar and Perry on the bass. "Wow, that was great. It was a bit out there, unusual, but I felt it came straight from the heart. I loved it!" Saly said, "However, I do have just a few remarks", he continued, "I do think the clarinet should be played by one of the boys, and we definitely need a piano." Jack objected as this was his clarinet, and he didn't like others to play it. However, that problem was solved by deciding that they would buy another clarinet, though the piano would have to wait for now. "The good thing is that 'When The Saints' is in the Public Domain, and no copyright is due anymore so, we can freely use it". Before leaving for Milano the next day, Saly made a long list of instructions, and he said he would send some more modern music for them to learn.

Back in Milano, Saly started to organise things. He told Susan that when the group was ready, he would send a bus. In the meantime, they trained very hard, mainly on what Saly had advised Susan to work on. Jack was happy to help Joshua practise with the new clarinet.

Many things had to be organised at home in their village. The Don, like a good friend once again, offered to help out. With everyone gone, the village needed to be kept secure somehow. Some of the houses needed locks on the doors, and Don organised that at short notice. He also arranged for a reliable person to go up there every so often to keep an eye out for unwelcome visitors and to switch on irrigation for the grapevines when it would become very hot and dry for the grapes. The Don said that he would do that himself as well.

Jack and Susan told the Don that they very much appreciated his help with everything but that they had no idea how long they would be away. Don Giovanni reassured them that he would look after things in their mountain village. They would keep in daily contact.

Chapter Twenty-Two

Then the big day came, and the group, accompanied by Jack and Susan, boarded the bus to Milano. Everyone was very excited to go on this adventure. When they arrived, the boys and girls feasted their eyes on the enormous and beautiful city. They didn't know where to look first! They marvelled at the hotel, with the marble steps, bell boys, waiters, room service and so on.

It was both overwhelming and unbelievable for them. There was so much to get used to. Ozie and Rosie shared a room. They would rather have shared with their boyfriends, Paul and Levy. However, disappointed as they were, things were organised that way.

The hotel's nightclub had a grand piano and was made available most days for the group to practise, which they did. A lot of hard work went into training and repetitions. It became apparent that not only could she sing, Rosie had a talent for playing the piano. She was a natural. She had blues and jazz in her blood and bones. Their impresario, Saly, was over the moon with that discovery.

Another big event for the group was when the tailors came to take their measurements for their stage costumes. The tailors came back within a week with the new outfits. Many sightseeing trips were organised as well, and the young African musicians were feasting their eyes, constantly and highly impressed by the beautiful cathedral and other churches and buildings.

Their first gig opportunity came when Saly received an invitation from the hotel management. 'Would The Monti Alto Group like to play at the nightclub bar of the hotel this weekend?' They would, and they did! Even if not all of their first official performance was appreciated by all, the gentle and slow jazz certainly was. They all looked great in their sparkly new stage outfits, with the girls looking especially spectacular.

Not long after that, Saly told them that the Vatican had planned a congress to support refugees, and that his application for the group to take part, had been accepted as this would be a good demonstration of what refugees or immigrants could bring to the country. Jack and Susan were very nervous and thought that the group was not ready for that yet. However, Saly was so full of confidence that David, who totally trusted Saly's judgement, was happy for them.

Their performance would be seen by a worldwide audience as the event would be televised globally. The group performed well at the event. It was brief, only one piece, but this would soon change.

An agitated show director came to Saly and nervously said, "I am in big trouble! We need your group! Please, can they play for another ten minutes? We have a problem and need to fill some time". Sally quickly went to see the group and said, "We need to play for another ten minutes. What shall we play? Come on guys, we have to go on stage. There is no time to think long about this!"

"Ok, come on Ozie, you sing", said Aron, and they both walked onto the stage; Aron started to play on his trumpet whilst

Ozie sang 'When The Saints Go Marching In'. Joshua followed him with the clarinet and then came Samuel with the trombone. Addo and Levy followed on the guitars. Benjamin slipped around the stage, gliding behind his drums like Rosie behind the piano. It became a huge success.

They all entered the stage, one by one, playing in sequence, and even Perry, on the bass, played a variety of the same melody. Each, in turn, received a big applause as they entered the stage. It was unbelievable; even the Pope was clapping with the rhythm, and all the cardinals followed. Those ten minutes passed before they knew it. This spontaneous fill-in-time resulted in 'The Monti Alto Group' becoming famous overnight.

On the bus back to Milano, the group talked non-stop about what had happened and the wondrous things they had seen in the holy city. The huge, beautiful buildings and statues every-where made an unforgettable impression on them. The members of the band had no idea that they were becoming famous, but when Benjamin overheard Saly and David speak of their ambitious plans, Benjamin said wistfully, "When we are rich and famous, I will send lots of money home". The others agreed to that.

Chapter Twenty-Three

Susan had concerns about the possibility and the consequences of the young musicians becoming successful and famous. She discussed this with Jack. What if the boys would become rich and famous? Saly already imagined the boys in Paris, London, New York, and, of course, Hollywood, but Susan was more concerned about what would become of her teenagers, so fresh from the countryside and speaking only basic English and, thanks to her teachings, a little Italian.

Jack suggested they organise an unscheduled sightseeing tour without the knowledge of their impresario and hire a bus to take the boys and girls through the worst slums of the town to show them what the other side of society was. They did, and on this tour, Jack explained to the young men that in Italy, just like in other places in the world, there were many poor people as there was much unemployment these days. Losing hope, many of those people sought relief by drinking and drugs. They observed people begging and a group of drunks fighting in front of a bar. "Please let what you see here be a lesson to you. Never give up hope, and keep searching for ways to improve your life and the life of others. Never,

ever start with drugs, not even as a little 'pick me up'. If disillusioned or depressed, think back on how you started", Jack pleaded.

In one of the smaller backstreets, a small car was parked near the middle of the road, and their bus couldn't pass. After a short while and many "Mamma Mia's" from Samuel, their designated driver, one of the stronger boys hopped off the bus and beckoned the others, "Come on, boys!"

Samuel, Ben, Samson and three of the others picked up the car and put it on the footpath under big applause from a bunch of bystanders. The boys laughed and bowed to them as if to say thank you!

Later that evening, when back in the hotel, Ben asked who would join him for an ice cream. Samson and Samuel went with him. The three walked to the next street where, just around the corner, there was a small stand where the delicious Italian ice cream, Gelato was sold. They did get the ice cream they chose, but they thought the change they received was wrong. The stallholder became somewhat agitated, but neither of the three friends could make sense of what he said. Then they just shrugged their shoulders and left.

Confused by this experience, they took a wrong turn. A few local young men, who had observed the situation, followed them. Soon after the boys discovered their mistake and turned around, they were confronted by the young men, who stopped them and demanded their money. But Ben and the other two were not going to oblige. They shook them off and tried to walk away. That's when one of the thugs hit Ben hard and started a fight which involved them all.

People appeared on their balconies and hung out of windows to watch the spectacle until the police showed up. The local boys blamed the 'African illegals' who should return to their own country and accused them of cheating the ice cream salesman. Ben and the others couldn't follow most of the exchanges nor make themselves understood.

The 'Polizia' told them to come with them to the station, but when one of them took hold of Ben's arm, he became very upset and pulled himself loose, resulting in a hit with the police baton. This caused Samson to floor the policeman with one strong swing of his left arm, but all three were swiftly handcuffed, bundled into a police vehicle and taken to the station, where they were locked up for the rest of the day and the following night.

When Saly found out where Ben and the other two were, he alerted Jack and Susan, who contacted David for help. It didn't take David long to get Ben, Samson and Samuel free, but it did become front-page news. Depending on which newspaper, it was reported that either the situation was caused by police brutality or the result of allowing illegal refugees into the country. However, the initiative of the Vatican to show that immigrants can be a great asset to the country and, subsequently, the performance at the Vatican, which had been shown on television all over the world, had helped 'The Monti Alto Group' become very popular. The fight was soon forgotten, and they received many more invitations. Their new celebrity status gave Saly the chance to organise the world tour he had imagined on the bus home from the Vatican.

For this, they had walked for months, often in life-threatening circumstances, and they had lost one of their best mates. Two things the famous 'Monti Alto Group' would never forget, no matter how busy they were, was to send money to their family in Southern Africa and to come home to Susan and Jack every year for grape harvest time and be with their saviours Jack and Susan in 'Valparaiso Vecchio', now named 'Monti Alto'.

The End